Introduction

Meet Monsieur Philippe, a charming, fine-mannered fox, whose story is now a legend in forest and farmyard. With cunning wit and swift, graceful movements, he snares his share of animals for his gourmet feasts. Killing rabbits and chickens, after all, is what foxes do.

But Monsieur Philippe, in addition to being an accomplished chef, has the soul of a poet and wonders if hunting small game must always be the only way for him. He finds the answer on a wonderful Christmas Eve.

The transformation of Monsieur Philippe demonstrates to children the true meaning of Christmas and shows what happens when we respond to the mystery of grace. Author Ethel Pochocki echoes the biblical prophecy that "the wolf will dwell with the lamb, the leopard will take rest with the kid, the calf and the lion cub will feed together, and a little child shall lead them" (Is 12:6).

This beautifully illustrated book is destined to become a favorite of young children everywhere as they learn the meaning of the coming of Christ.

The Editors

ETHEL FRANCES POCHOCKI is a freelance writer of children's books, stories and poetry. Her stories have been published in *Pockets, Cricket, St. Anthony Messenger* and *The Christian Science Monitor.* Among her many books are *Grandma Bagley Leads the Way* (Augsburg/Fortress), *The Attic Mice* and *Rosebud and Red Flannel* (Henry Holt), and *Saints for the Seasons* (St. Anthony Messenger Press).

©1990 by Ave Maria Press, Notre Dame, IN 46556

International Standard Book Number: 0-87793-431-2

Library of Congress Catalog Card Number: 90-82095

Cover design by Elizabeth J. French

Printed and Bound in the United States of America.

The Fox Who Found Christmas

Ethel Frances Pochocki

Illustrated by Thomas P. Bell

AVE MARIA PRESS
Notre Dame, Indiana 46556

Once, a long time ago in the old forest, something strange happened on Christmas Eve. Happily strange it was, but puzzling, nonetheless. It has grown into a legend among the animals, and to this day, they tell it to the little ones on the holy night.

It has to do with one of their own, Monsieur (that's French for Mr.) Philippe, a fox of high esteem. He exemplified the best of the fox-character—a brilliant, cunning wit, exquisite manners, charming humor, and in all his movements, a delicate grace. It was a joy to watch him fence or dance a minuet.

He also had a touch of the poet in his soul—an eye for truth and beauty in all that he encountered. He revered all life, even the animals he felt bound to kill.

He did not understand why this was so, only that it was. "Life is a mystery," he would sigh, as he looked to the night sky and the world beyond the stars.

Monsieur Philippe was also a cook of great artistry. When he gave a party, everybody came. He knew where to find the herbs and blossoms for wine, the wild leeks and mushrooms for his rabbit stew and chicken and dumplings, the tiny crabapples for fritters, and caraway seeds for cookies.

When the moon rose, he picked the young peas and beans and onions, while the cats and dogs and humans slept.

And then, swift and deadly as an arrow, he caught the chickens and rabbits for his famous feasts. He told himself that this was just part of being a fox. It was the way he must follow, he had no choice. Robins eat worms, cats eat robins, foxes eat chickens and rabbits. It was the way. And so he kept on stalking and catching and killing and cooking.

But as the years passed, he yearned less and less to stalk his prey and end their lives with one quick movement. He would much rather sit in the tall grass and enjoy the antics of the foolish chickens and scatter-brained rabbits.

"If only I could change the way," he would sigh, before he bagged his meal for the evening.

And so it was, this night before Christmas, that Monsieur Philippe set out in air as crisp and brittle as an icicle. He picked some wild grapes hanging from vines he could reach and cranberries from the bog. They were a bit shrivelled from the cold but would be delicious in a sauce for his lemon-garlic chicken.

He sang softly to himself and the steam from his breath rose like wispy grace notes.

"*A fox went out on a chilly night.*
He prayed the moon for it to give him light . . ."

He needed no moon for light, he thought, for every star in the universe was like a jewel on display in the black velvet sky, burning silver bright, twinkling, winking; some even seemed to turn to gold if one stared at them long enough.

Monsieur Philippe, in his white gloves and red plaid scarf, his basket of woven willow strips over his arm, stood on the small hill at the edge of the forest and looked up at the stars for a long while.

He thought of all the years the stars had looked down upon the forests and the foxes before him . . . what stories they could tell! Did they shine as bright on the first Christmas as they did this night?

What must it have been like? He had heard from a storyteller who had passed through the old forest that on this special night, all the animals were friends, that they could talk and sing and give praise as the humans did.

He would have liked that—one night when he would not have to kill or cause pain or skulk off like a murderer. Of course, he quickly reassured himself, he was not a murderer. He was acting according to his nature. Wasn't he?

One star seemed to grow stronger as he watched it, almost blinding him. He felt compelled to stare deeply into it, into the fiery center.

And there in its golden fire he saw an image.

A small child lay in a manger, bathed in golden rays coming from a hole in the heavens. Around the crude bed knelt the animals of the farm and woods and jungle. A huge proud lion stood at the head of the manger above the child, as if he were the figurehead on a boat. Wolves, lambs, squirrels, mourning doves, a goose, an owl, rabbits, all smiled at him and each other. A black-and-white cat purred at his feet, and a dozen baby chicks spilled out from his hands. Monsieur Philippe stood transfixed, smiling back.

But then a great sadness came upon him. He saw no fox at the manger. "Why?" he asked. "Cannot a fox feel and love and adore as well as a wolf?"

"Why" he asked again, feeling tears rise, "am I not there?"

The child heard the question in Monsieur Philippe's heart. Through the dark reaches of space the child whispered his message of love. "We are all brothers. Love me as I love you. Love one another as I love you."

At first the fox did not understand. But soon the warmth of the child's voice touched his heart and made it so light that he felt as if 100 balloons were inside his body. He wanted to leap and dance and sing. Could it be that simple? Just *love*?

The vision of the child and animals faded into the
brightness of the star. But from within it the fox heard
laughter and singing as sweet and light as a breeze teasing
glass wind chimes. He longed to be part of that joy.

"You can change your way," sang his heart.
"Take a different path. Be his brother."

As he stood there, not knowing how to do this, he saw a large white ball moving toward him, crazily charging like a snow plow across the open field. The moon cast the shadow of large haunches and feet, flattened ears, a body leaping high into the air.

Suddenly, Achille, the largest snowshoe rabbit in the forest, stopped and froze. His heart almost stopped beating, for many of his relatives had contributed to Monsieur Philippe's culinary reputation.

"So this is how it will end," said Achille to himself, not daring to move even his eyes. There was no way he could escape the fox, who was now so close the hare could feel his breath. His loved ones would wait in vain for him to come home, but he would not come. He would be the fox's Christmas dinner instead.

The fox bowed to Achille. "*Bon soir* (that's French for good evening), my friend Achille. Is it not a lovely, starry night? I wish you and yours a happy celebration. *Bon soir!*" He bowed again and continued on his way, his scarf blowing behind him in the rising wind.

He stopped by a jack-o-lantern inhabited by a family of mice. The pumpkin's features had softened from a fierce scowl to a sunken quizzical look, not unpleasant. Through the windows, which had been the pumpkin's eyes, he saw the mouse children trimming the tiny tree and the father and mother roasting acorns over a fire of cedar shavings.

He felt another pang. Oh to be part of a family, warm and snug inside their little world! A tender feeling for them—was it love?—spread through him. He wanted to protect them and keep their lives forever contented. Dear little creatures! He could imagine them scampering over the hay of the manger, too quick for even the child to catch.

He went on, for he was in a hurry to reach the henhouse before midnight. He had made a good beginning. He had bowed to Achille and made pleasantries with him; he had loved the mice from afar. Now, giddy with newfound joy, he would dare to act in the most unfox-like manner. He would visit the chickens, wish them *Joyeux Noel* (that's French for Merry Christmas), and leave with his basket empty. He sang again and danced in tune,

> *"Fox ran 'til he came to the farmer's bin,*
> *Where the ducks and geese were kept therein,"*

as he followed the well-worn path to the henhouse.

Laughter and whispers and singing came from within, and above it all, the loud, shrill clucking of buxom Madame (that's French for Mrs.) Sylvie, the mother of the little brood of chicks (six daughters, one son).

The door, hung with a wreath of balsam and strawflowers, was slightly ajar, and Monsieur Philippe, not quite sure of what he should do, stood listening.

"Come, come, children," said Madame Sylvie shrilly, "it's getting late, and your mother is tired even if you aren't. Gather round—Estelle, you're spilling your popcorn, take care!—and I'll tell you the story of the first Christmas and the rooster who was the first to spread the good news to the shepherds. The humans think the angels did it, but *we* know better!"

The shadow of Monsieur Philippe, who had gently pushed the door open upon the loving scene, fell across the room and covered the baby chicks like a dark blanket.

Madame Sylvie turned quickly and gave a shriek.

"No, not tonight, not this sacred night! How could the child allow the dreaded enemy to strike tonight?"

She had lost many of her brothers and sisters to him—now would he take her little ones also? Anger wiped out fear, and in her outrage she spoke boldly to the fox. "Monsieur Philippe," for of course she knew who he was, "how dare you spoil this holy eve? Have you no manners, no respect for the child? Do you not have a heart as well as a stomach? How can you kill on Christmas Eve?!"

The little chicks cheeped and ran under her skirt for safety.

"Madame Sylvie," answered the fox, "I come only to wish you well this night, and to bring you this small gift. Consider me, if you will, a solitary Wise Man." He emptied his basket of the wild grapes and cranberries at her feet.

Madame Sylvie looked deep into the fox's eyes and said nothing. She was a wise creature who knew that life was a mystery. "This could be a clever ruse," she thought. "Then again, it might not be." If it were, they would all die. If it were not, then life was even more mysterious than she had imagined. In either case, she would not be guilty of bad manners.

"It is most kind of you to remember us, sir. Children, say *thank you* to Monsieur Philippe." The chicks came out from under her skirt, cheeping in delight over such unexpected delicacies that came from beyond their world of a fenced-in yard. "And you, Monsieur, will you accept some small gifts from us in return?"

She went into her kitchen and brought out a bag of dried mushrooms, a pot of chives, a small round of goat's cheese, six brown eggs, and a small jar of yellow syrup. "For your Christmas dinner; and the ginger syrup is my mother's recipe, good for colds and an upset stomach."

They bowed to each other and said good night, and the fox, carrying his precious gifts with care, danced his way home by the light of the stars.

On the cold and frosty Christmas Day, he baked a cheese omelet so elegant, so delicious, the like of which has not been tasted before or since. It was a miracle omelet which seemed to have no end, for it fed all who came to the feast.

We do not know if this happened every Christmas Day thereafter, or if Monsieur Philippe was moved by love just this once. All we know is that it happened, and that life is a mystery.